DR. IMMORTELLE

BY

KATHLEEN LUDWICK

British Library Cataloguing-in-Publication Data
A catalogue record for this book is available from
the British Library

GOTHIC

' "Gothic" implies a style of writing, a way of looking at things, a sense of "innocent horror". This classic tale of "vampirism" has all these ingredients along with a villain who is as much an innocent victim of Dr Immortelle as any of the children who they prey upon!'

Amazing Stories, 1930.

DR IMMORTELLE

by Kathleen Ludwick

I have to smile when I hear all this talk about rejuvenation, after the story Victor De Lyle told me, lying white and still on his cot in the hospital overlooking the ocean, the changing expression of his great dark eyes the only sign of life about him. Dr Immortelle beat them to it by about a hundred and fifty years. Strange that his theory has never occurred to any of our modern Occidental practitioners, at least not until very recently. I saw an item in the papers the other day that caused me to suspect that a European scientist had either discovered the secret for himself or perhaps gained his inspiration from the writing of the ancient alchemists, where no doubt Immortelle gained his.

I do not doubt that Methuselah lived a thousand years; I do not doubt that, barring accident, it is possible for men to live *ten thousand* years, if they so desire, or that men have done so and will do so again. Perhaps in time, longevity like that will become so universal as to be taken for granted. The process of rejuvenation will become as common as that of vaccination or the injection of the various serums and anti-toxins that are now the fad of the hour. It may even become compulsory by due process of law! It will follow naturally that the Mrs Sangsters (sic) of that day will be heard with respect and no doubt Malthus will have many statues erected to his memory.

Why shouldn't we be rejuvenated? Most of us have attained to but the vaguest conception of the meaning of life when 'the black camel kneels before the gate'. We hear a great deal about infant mortality, and it is indeed a pitiful thing: but the mortality of the mentally immature is also appalling and infinitely more tragic. But – goat's glands! The thought gives one a feeling of nausea. I wonder if the results of that same operation in olden times, as the historians say, 'shrouded by the mists of antiquity', do not form some basis for the legends of fauns and satyrs, those strange beings, half man and half goat, which figure so largely in Grecian and Latin mythology; and if, perhaps, the increasing number of such monsters did not result in the discontinuance of the operation? How shocking to become the parent of such a being! Thank heaven, there is another and better way! At least it will be better if there is wide and general knowledge concerning it for the protection of humanity. To the dissemination of such knowledge I now devote the last days of my life. For myself I do not desire longevity. Such a desire died in me when a Red Cross tent was bombed on the French frontier. Perhaps it was for this that I came, alive, out of the hell of the Argonne!

I have none of the arts of the professional writer. I know nothing of the rules of short-story writing. I am just a plain mining engineer of mediocre ability, wielding a geological pick and hammer more easily than a pen and more familiar with mortars than metaphors. I could run a tunnel to tap a ledge in a porphyry dike easier than I could tell this strange tale. I know more about secondary enrichments than I do of the terminology and equipment of modern surgery, but if the layman can grasp my meaning, I shall be well content. Often, strangely enough, it would seem, it is the man in the street who anticipates the most astounding scientific discoveries and grasps their tremendous significance to humanity before his apparent intellectual superiors. I realise that, as Walt Whitman said of his poems, 'It will do good – it may do much evil also'. But I have faith to believe that the good will far outweigh the evil.

I started for San Francisco one May evening from my parents' home in the Santa Cruz Mountains. It was a moonlit night, and there was little traffic on the highway. The air was soft and mild and fragrant with the scent of innumerable flowers in the gardens of the homes that line the highway down the Peninsula for half-a-hundred miles. Even the humblest home in this favored region may possess the never-ending joy of flowers the year around, if nothing more than the humble petunia and the cheerful scarlet geranium. Where on the face of the globe, except on the shores of the Mediterranean, is there another section so favored by nature as that to which the inhabitants of the region bordering on San Francisco Bay all pridefully refer to as 'The Peninsula'? It is the Mecca of the whole Pacific Coast. From the north they 'go down to the Bay to get warm', from the sunny San Joaquin, and further south, they stream up to the Bay 'to cool off'!

Eastward towered the dark bulk of Mount Diablo. To my right the waters of the lower bay flashed in the moonlight. On my left rose green, gently sloping hills, with their wealth of native shrubs and trees and their plantations of eucalyptus, reminding me always of those words of Howells':

'The inscrutable sadness of the mute races of trees.'

I passed Palo Alto with its picturesque university buildings, silent witness to the good that the tragedy of one life may bring to countless multitudes; the salt heaps of Leslie shone white as snow in the moonlight as I passed. It pleased me to speculate on the appearance of the section I was traversing, when it should have been settled as long as London or Paris or Naples has been.

And so I neared the twin cities of San Mateo and Burlingame, the latter with its picturesque little railroad station. A couple of miles south of San Mateo I almost ran over a woman carrying a suitcase. I stopped and offered her a ride. Imagine my astonishment when I found it was Linnie Chaumelle. I had known her as a child in Idaho and she had grown into the loveliest woman I have ever seen. I had long ago lost all track of the Chaumelles, but a few months previously had chanced to meet Linnie at the bedside of a friend in a local hospital, where she was on duty as a special nurse, and we had renewed our acquaintance.

It was the death of Linnie's little brother, Vernon, that precipitated the exposure of that strange and sinister being, Albert Immortelle, and his assistant, Victor de Lyle, and caused them to flee from the Wood River Valley 'between two days'. Immortelle asserted that the child had cut himself and he had dressed the wound. Linnie's uncle, an eastern surgeon of some note, arrived unexpectedly for a visit about that time. An infection developed and the child died. The child's uncle openly charged that the wound had been made by a surgeon, and that Immortelle had been performing an experiment of some sort. The Chaumelles were amongst the oldest residents of that section and highly respected. Feeling ran high and threats of lynching were openly uttered. Immortelle and his assistant owned one of the first automobiles in that section. They fled in the night, and in spite of the attention excited by the appearance of autos at that time, nothing was ever heard of them again until they reappeared many years later in San Francisco.

The strangest feature of it was that my own father stoutly affirmed that he had known Dr Immortelle some forty years before and he had appeared no older at the time he left Wood River Valley. Dr Immortelle insisted that he was the son of the physician my father had known, but father was positive in his identification. And to complicate matters still further, my grandfather declared that *he* had known this same Immortelle *sixty* years before! That he recognised him because of a peculiar triangular scar above one eyebrow. Dr Immortelle asserted that this scar was a family mark – a matter of heredity: but my grandfather had served in the Civil War and knew something about wounds himself. He laughed at the idea that the scar was a hereditary mark. As he said it, it was very unlikely that a grandfather and son and grandson should have been wounded in such a manner as to result in the same identical sort of scar in the same location. Moreover, the same explanation could not apply to Victor de Lyle. Both my grandfather and my father were willing to swear to his identity, so he could not be explained away so easily. The people of the camp were frankly puzzled. Both my grandfather and my father were men of unquestioned veracity whose sanity had never been doubted; hardheaded business men of good judgement and common sense. There was some mystery here. For those still living, it will be solved if they chance to read this narrative.

No words of mine could convey a just impression of Linnie's beauty and womanly grace; she was the ideal nurse, with the physique and vitality that every nurse should possess; and besides, she possessed that dignity and nobility of character in which many nurses are sadly lacking. To meet her in such a place, at such an hour, staggering under the weight of a heavy suitcase, and in what I might almost call a disheveled condition, was inexpressibly shocking to me. She was a woman of very even temperament, but she appeared to be labouring under considerable excitement. She asked me to drive her to her apartment in the city: but after hearing a part of her story I turned the car and drove back down the Peninsula – past Los Gatos and through the canyon, to the ranch of my parents in the Santa Cruz Hills. Linnie's mother and mine had been friends in those long-past Idaho days and I knew my mother would give her the care she needed. I left her there and returned to the city.

The afternoon papers were filled with the details of the latest accident in El Diablo Canyon. Dr Immortelle, a well-known local physician, and his associate, Victor de Lyle, had been conducting a sort of orphanage or sanitarium at Crescent Beach. Starting for the city at night, they had gone over the bank, into the canyon, hundreds of feet below. The accident had apparently been caused by their swerving the car to avoid running over the body of a tramp that some other car had struck and killed. Dr Immortelle had been killed instantly and shockingly mangled, and Victor de Lyle had been fatally injured.

One of the puzzling features of the accident had been the presence of a woman's footprints near the scene of the tragedy; also the appearance of a young and beautiful woman at a little station down the Peninsula, who had appeared greatly agitated at missing the last local to the city and had started out afoot, carrying a heavy suitcase, apparently with the intention of walking to the next station two or three miles away, to catch the inter-urban car whose terminus was at that point. The theory was advanced that the footprints had been made by a woman occupant of the car that had struck the tramp; that, getting out of the machine, she had found the tramp to be fatally injured, and because of this and possibly other compromising circumstances, she had feared to inform the authorities. The mystery was never solved to the satisfaction of the police and detectives. Only one person besides myself and parents, and the actual actors in the tragedy, ever knew who made those footprints. That was my wife. Linnie made them – Linnie, my other self, who sleeps in a little French cemetery near where the Germans bombed the Red Cross tent where she tended the wounded and dying. I promised Victor de Lyle that I would write this story as best I could, but it would not have been given to the world in her lifetime had my wife lived. I am giving it to the world now because the time for my own passing draws near and I believe the world is ready for the wide and practical application of Dr Immortelle's method of rejuvenation.

I went to see Victor de Lyle as soon as the physicians would allow me to do so. There were certain features of Linnie's story that I desired to have corroborated. Bit by bit, at the cost of the most excruciating agony, the recital spread over many days, he told me the most amazing story I have ever heard. There have been times since when I have wondered if I weren't as locoed as any Idaho steer that has been browsing on rattleweed: and then I remembered finding Linnie on the highway, and what my father and grandfather said about having known Immortelle so many years before, and thereby regain faith in my own sanity.

As a child I had always feared Dr Immortelle, the sinister-looking older man with the dark, compelling eyes, despite his efforts to win my favor: but I had always liked his young assistant, De Lyle, with the ready, sympathetic smile and gentle manners and the kind brown eyes whose expression hinted of sorrow and tragedy. I wrote down his story as he related it to me day by day. Later I read it to him and he pronounced the most vital portions correct in every detail. Since then I have consulted various authorities, talked with physicians and surgeons of international reputation, and I am assured there is no serious technical error in the tale.

I can differentiate between lancet and scapula, bistoury and cannula; I can even discuss the merits of the Aveling syringe as compared with the Collins apparatus or Spencer's instrument with the cannula that can be plunged directly into the blood-vessel. Also, I have opinions as to the merits of arterial as opposed to intravenous transfusion: but I had hard work learning to twist my tongue around such terms as phlebotomy, arteriovenous anastomosis, ambolism and thrombosis: and it was a long time before I got hep to the difference between Crile's tube and Payre's tube and Brewster's tube of German silver. This, then, is what de Lyle told me.

'I was born a slave on a plantation in North Carolina in the year 1745. No, *not* 1845. I was born a mulatto. Perhaps you think my mind is affected – but wait till I have finished! My father was a white overseer and my mother a negress from the Guinea Coast. I am not delirious – I am not insane

– although I realise that it must be difficult for you to credit my statements.' Incredulously I noted his soft, waving brown hair, his hazel eyes, his skin that in health had been fairer than my own suntanned hide. 'You will believe me before my story is ended,' he said sardonically. I did.

'My old master was of French ancestry. Huguenot stock. His wife's people were Pennsylvania Dutch – and Quakers. They were in one of the great treks from Pennsylvania to North Carolina. She had not hesitated to marry outside the faith in which she had been reared when she met and fell in love with the elder Immortelle. Perhaps it was from her that Albert inherited that mystical tendency which influenced his life so greatly.

'The elder Immortelle was the proprietor of a large plantation. Naturally, he grew the products peculiar to that region – tobacco, cotton, corn and horses. He had been educated for a physician but he had a passion for stock raising. Being an altruist, his knowledge of medicine and the crude surgery of the times was of incalculable benefit to the inhabitants of that sparsely settled region, and he gave of his time and services as freely to the most wretched slave as to the haughty proprietor of the most widely stretching plantation. He possessed one of the finest libraries in America at that time. Among his books were some of the works of the ancient Alchemists. They possessed a strange fascination for his son. The boy would pore over them for hours when other lads of his age were engaged in riding or hunting or other local sports and pleasures usual to youths of their years.

'Second only to his interest in books was the attraction animals possessed for him, especially his father's thorough-bred herd. Even as a child he was always begging for pets. As he grew older, he would ask for them under the condition that they were to be his own exclusive property to do with as he pleased. His father was greatly pleased by the scientific spirit which Albert displayed in the breeding of the stock on the plantation. My master possessed some of the best specimens of horseflesh in that section. He fondly hoped to see his son become one of the most famous stockbreeders of his day. If he had suspected the object which no doubt inspired his son even at an early age, his emotions would have been of a different character.

'Albert turned his earliest attention to the breeding of

poultry, cats, dogs, sheep and other comparatively short-lived animals, that he might observe the results of certain experiments on several generations. He was especially impressed with the disastrous results of inbreeding in relation to fecundity, and this formed the very basis of the theory he was slowly evolving and which was to be fraught with such tragic and momentous results to himself and countless others.

'Like most Southern gentlemen of that period, he was fond of gaming, wine and women: but so great was his self-control that I never knew him to overstep the bounds of sobriety. In gaming and the pursuit of women his methods were cold-bloodedly scientific; but I believe that during his whole lifetime he really loved only one woman.

'He was selfish and cruel, persistent in the pursuit of any object. He was a "throwback", a reversion to some strange type that one found it impossible to associate with either parent. His father and mother never understood him. He was an even greater puzzle to me who saw more of him than anyone else did. We were nearly the same age. His father had given me to him for his own personal attendant. It seems strange to you that I was ever a slave, doesn't it? But I assure you that it is true and I am able to verify this statement in every respect. I was his almost constant companion. For hours at a time he would pore over certain problems whose existence I did not at that time suspect. I have known few human beings capable of such intense concentration.

'When we were young lads he said to me once:

' "Victor, when I will move my hand, why is it that my hand responds to my will? It must be for the reason that every smallest particle of that hand has a consciousness of its own!" And this was long before Dalton had advanced his atomic theory. We had never heard of molecules or atoms, to say nothing of electrons! He had no modern microscope to aid in confirming his theories. No one at that time had ever witnessed the marvelous division of cells, the orderly action of centrosomes and chromosomes with which every student of histology is today acquainted and takes as a matter of course. His error lay in his theory of the manner of reproduction of cells and yet, in spite of this, he and I are, or were, living witnesses to the success of his experimentation.

'He acquired all that the colonies had to offer at that period in the study of medicine and surgery, then pursued his studies in London and Paris and even in other capitals of Europe. I remember once in Vienna – but let that pass! I accompanied him always and for his own purposes he educated me. There never was the same prejudice on the Continent against colored people that has always existed here in America.

'We were in Paris at the outbreak of the Revolutionary War. A privateer nearly captured us on our way home. I have often wished that it had sunk us. Albert served through the war and I was with him as his personal attendant. Naturally, we were exposed to great dangers. I feel certain now that he was by nature cowardly, but his scientific bent of mind and the goal he had in view were sufficient to counterbalance his fears. He had the reputation of being one of the most fearless and efficient surgeons in the Continental Army. Strange that a man should so determinedly face death in his efforts to find a preventive of Death itself! How many revolutionary heroes lost their lives as a result of his experiments I have no means of knowing, but the total was doubtless large. I possessed a considerable knowledge of medicine and surgery, myself, for those times, which was all a part of my master's plans. He took great pains to instruct me in the anatomy of the nerves and blood-vessels.

'At the close of the war we settled in New York. We took a house in a secluded suburban section. Immortelle was then about forty years old and both of us commenced to feel the effects of years of military service with the inescapable hardships which would appear so incredibly severe to modern soldiers. My master's step was not so springy as it had been.

'Never have I seen a human being who dreaded the approach of age as did my master. It was while we were living in the New York house that he first broached the subject that must have been uppermost in his thoughts for years. I was astounded. His plans to make practical application of his theories filled me with horror, hardened to suffering as I had become during the course of the war. I am by nature conservative. Also, I had not the depth of intellect of Albert Immortelle, nor his scientific bent of mind.

'Afterwards, I could recall many hints and innuendoes

that should have prepared me for his disclosure and I wondered that I had not grasped his purpose sooner. Cleverly he dangled the bait before me.

' "Remember," he would say when I wavered, "only accident can bar us from attaining any age we may desire to reach. We can remain youthful and grow increasingly attractive with the passage of the years, instead of hideously ugly with wrinkled skins and bald heads and the yellow snags of age in our mouths that ever repel youth and beauty." (Our dentists at that day were not capable of performing the miracles of artistic dental surgery that we take as a matter of course today.)

'Remember, he was my master – I his slave. Over me he had the power of life and death. Never was such a cunning tempter. He tempted me with the promise of freedom and the hope that through the gradual loss of most of my own blood, covering a long period of time, and the substitution of Caucasian blood through the process of transfusion, I might, to all intents and purposes, become a Caucasian. You cannot understand what that means, you who have not been an object of contempt and disdain through no fault of your own; you who have not been jostled brutally on the sidewalk and kicked off the curb by your actual inferiors, and felt yourself helpless to resent brutality and insult!

'Briefly, his theory was this: That the tiny particles of our bodies which we now call cells, breed and reproduce their kind in a manner somewhat similar to that of most animals; that the inbreeding through countless generations, in the body of a human being which they themselves compose, causes a loss in fecundity just as it does in horses and cattle; causes the cells to degenerate, to "run out", as we say of animals and plants; *and that this loss in fecundity is the true cause of old age.* He believed that, as stock men range far afield for new strains to strengthen the breeds of their flocks and herds, so new vigor might be acquired by introducing young and vigorous cells into the blood of the aged. *Necessarily, the cells to be so introduced must be from the vascular system of youth;* and even then, I think, he glimpsed the truth which science has but lately demonstrated, that the character of the blood of an individual becomes fixed at the age of three or four years and thereafter remains constant.

'There is no doubt that the ancient Alchemists practiced this method of rejuvenation. Immortelle's error lay in his theory as to the manner of reproduction of the cells, which, instead of breeding with older cells in the veins of the recipient, simply mutiplied through division in their new locations crowding out the weaker cells, and went about their tasks of rebuilding the body with new materials and removing the waste products.

'Tranfusion is old – how old no man can say. It was probably practiced long before recorded history. A friend of mine who has accompanied several archeological expeditions to the Far East asserts that the Alchemists gained their knowledge from the secret records of a fraternity old before Babylon and Nineveh became but rubbish heaps covered by the shifting desert sands! It is a fact that transfusion was employed in the case of Pope Innocent VII, and there is a tradition to the effect that three young boys perished in the attempt. Perhaps the old legends of vampirism had their origin in such a source.

'Transfusion is a common operation today, but when Albert Immortelle first broached the subject to me, an open announcement of our object would have been regarded with the greatest horror and only too well-founded fear of results would have rendered it impossible for us to secure subjects. Anesthetics had not yet been discovered and aseptic surgery was a hundred years in the future. We had to devise ways and means of securing subjects.

'It was my young master's plan to found an orphanage, whose most promising inmates he would later use for his transfusion experiments, which heretofore had included animals only. I was to be his first subject after the children; and when I had mastered the details of the process, he himself would submit to the operation. Of course, the danger as well as the suffering was incalculably greater than in these days of anesthetics and aseptic surgery. My master was skilled in the art of hypnotism, or mesmerism, as it was then called, but it often failed. Probably he was the first surgeon to use that strange force for anesthetisation. It is a well-known fact that children are less susceptible to it than adults; and our subjects were all children, mostly of tender years – in fact all that *survived* were of such tender age! Tales of children of such age would in any event be treated as due to vivid imaginations. Even to this day I sometimes waken from nightmares with the agonised screams of those little victims ringing in my ears.

'Today there is practically no danger from infection and the danger from clotting is being eliminated through the division of humanity into groups classified according to the constituency of their blood. We had no aspirating syringe to determine the amount of blood taken from the donors and how many little victims lost their lives in this manner, as sacrifices to our rejuvenation, I have no means of knowing. It was, of course, unwise to keep records of such cases. All I know is that there were many fatalities. How we escaped with our own lives is a mystery to me. I am unable to fathom the inscrutable purpose of Providence in allowing us to cumber this earth for so long a time.

'When my conscience revolted, always before my eyes Immortelle dangled the bait of my own altered personality; for I had emerged, a radiant Caucasian, from my somber and repellent negroid chrysalis. As far as I am personally concerned, from a physical standpoint, I am, or rather was, a living witness to the success of his experiment. Even the most widely experienced ethnologist would hardly suspect me of having one drop of negro blood in my veins. No one who had known me as a kinky-haired mulatto youth, were he in existence still, would ever recognise that colored boy in the cultured, refined Caucasian with the waving brown hair, hazel eyes and complexion as fair as your own, with the rosy hue of health in his cheeks. From a selfish and brutal young savage with a violent temper, I had been transformed into an amiable and tractable individual, vastly useful to my master, but more conscientious than was conducive to my peace of mind or his. This was due, I am sure, to Immortelle's deliberate selection of children of most amiable disposition for donors in transfusion operations in which I was the recipient. For himself he always selected fearless and intrepid subjects of indomitable wills. Such wills are often characteristic of amiable children. Stubbornness and strength of will differ from each other as widely as the poles.

'For the sake of greater safety, to be more reasonably certain that the blood of the donor would assimilate with my own, Immortelle always bled me freely before a transfusion. Immortelle deserves credit at least for his scientific accomplishments. Intellectually he was a giant amongst the men of his time. When he commenced his experiments he had no safe and sure scientific ground beneath his feet. He was treading the insecure and shifting sands of conjecture.

'Always he emphasised the ultimate benefit to humanity of our experiments; but for many a long and lonely year I realised that his own chief object was to live as long as possible, in order to gratify his sensual appetites, however Epicurean they might have been termed, to the limit of danger to his hold on life.

'Every man with a drop of blood in his veins has a passionate desire for offspring. Several times I contemplated marriage, but Albert always discouraged me.

'He argued that if we married and had families, we must either witness the passing from life of our wives and offspring, or witness their endurance of the sufferings and dangers of transfusion. We knew nothing of aseptic surgery, but I believe my master grasped the principles of it before we commenced our experiments, for he always used bottled water and the scorched linen dressings that so many regarded merely as a superstition of old midwives.

'There was always the danger of thrombosis due to the admixture of certain bloods which refused to assimilate. Immortelle argued with good grounds for his conviction, that it would be impossible to rejuvenate our wives and offspring even to the second generation, without knowledge of our methods becoming known. Someone amongst such a large group would inevitably give the secret away. Also when a hue and cry were raised, as was bound to be the case sooner or later, it would be difficult, if not impossible, to escape from popular wrath with a large number of relatives and dependents. It had been difficult enough on several occasions for our two selves. So reluctantly I relinquished my dream of conjugal felicity – the tender joys of one's own fireside, for the Dead Sea fruit of immortality in the flesh. I realised my error many long years ago: for I have come to know that immortality for the individual isolated from his kind could not atone for the loss of the happiness conferred by a perfect and harmonious union and the sweet delights afforded by the companionship of one's own offspring.

'Of course it was impossible to conduct an orphanage without attendants, and more especially female attendants. Ours were chiefly young women who had been saved by Immortelle and myself. They were obviously curious when assisting at transfusion operations, but their curiosity was never satisfied. The trained nurse had not as yet been evolved when we commenced our experiments in rejuvenation.

'Naturally all our philanthropic efforts to save the reputations of the erring were not successful. Usually they covered their tracks in coming to us and always bore an assumed name. When they departed, only Immortelle and I knew how, or when, or what their destination was. We had many aliases, he and I, but used our own names most frequently. It was embarrassing to meet people one had perhaps known forty years before. In such cases, he often passed for a son of himself, as in Idaho, where, however, he failed to deceive your father.

'In spite of all, suspicion would fasten on us. Rumors would spread connecting us with various mysterious disappearances. We found it expedient to leave our New York address on one occasion, more hastily than was convenient. So it was with our Philadelphia orphanage and others we established in this country. It was the same with those we established in London, and in Paris and other Continental cities. In some locations we spent as long a period as ten years. In others no sooner were we established than some catastrophe would occur, which would spoil all our plans and send us scurrying into hiding. This was the case when we were compelled to depart so hastily from that quiet and comparatively isolated valley in Idaho, where you and I first met – you a child and I to all appearances a young and inexperienced physician, but in reality an old and saddened man with experience of agonies unparalleled by any other person save my master, Immortelle! On him they had apparently no effect.

'In that little Idaho mining camp everything seemed favorable to our plans. It was a small camp and yet not small enough to allow each resident to become extremely familiar with the private affairs of all the rest. There was a considerable floating population, as in all mining camps, which was an advantage from our point of view.

'The absolute privacy essential to the successful prosecution of our plans was possible in the house we chose amongst the magnificent old cottonwoods of the river bottom and from which that beautiful but brawling stream derives its name. Earth does not hold a more picturesque spot than that narrow valley walled in by the precipitous mountains of the Sawtooth range. Often I close my eyes to see quite vividly again those miles on miles of cottonwoods. I recall the contrast of their orange hues in autumn with the dark green of the hardy firs that venture bravely down into the valley so far from most of their kind, and I see the thousands of ears of flame-colored chokecherry brush. And in the early summer, who that has ever seen them can forget those acres upon acres of blue forget-me-nots? In that valley they seem to disregard their naturally retiring habits that lead them to choose their abodes in the shelter of trees and shrubs. Away from all shelter, they boldly advance into the valley and flaunt their vivid hues under the blue skies of Idaho!

'Our house, as you remember, was an old, flimsy, unpainted weatherbeaten structure, but easily and cheaply remodeled for our purpose, ostensibly that of residence and laboratory. Immortelle was supposed to be deeply interested in the study of chemistry. Naturally, in such a climate, where the cold is so intense for a long period of each year, deep cellars are indispensable. We constructed a large one, also an underground laboratory with double skylight and heavy shutters which would prevent freezing of our chemicals and also serve to muffle any undesirable sounds and outcries.

'The river bottom consisted chiefly of gravel in which a small grave might easily and rapidly be dug at dead of night, if necessary. Also, the cottonwoods and thickets of wild roses, chokecherries and other shrubs hung with the creepers of the wild clematis, screened us in summer from inquisitive eyes and permitted easy access to a certain disreputable quarter of the camp. It was always possible in case of urgent necessity to secure assistance from this quarter, for there are always some nurses amongst those unfortunates. Dr Immortelle never passed up anything. In return for his professional services he was usually able to obtain assistance that was almost as invaluable as his own. We were acquainted with the details of many a tragedy hidden from the knowledge of the general public. As you may know, it was the discovery by two little girls of the grave of a newborn infant, richly clad, in the gravel of the river bottom, together with the death of little Vernon Chaumelle, that precipitated our flight.

'There never was any necessity, from a financial standpoint, for Dr Immortelle or myself to practice our professions. The proceeds from the sale of his father's plantation, to which he was the only heir, had been invested in Manhattan real estate nearly a hundred years before, as well as my own salary after the Emancipation Proclamation. The doctor's profession was only a blind, only a cloak for our real and sinister purposes.

'A considerable space of time is naturally required to establish a physician in a new location. Immortelle usually employed some length of time in judiciously cultivating the acquaintance of the local "four hundred", many of whom, sooner or later, he was absolutely certain, would require his professional services. It fell to my lot to make the acquaintance of the oldest inhabitants and, through them, to familiarise myself with the history of the best of families, chiefly in regard to heredity, persistently recurring physical characteristics and freedom from blood taint of a certain character.

'The densely wooded river bottom furnished an ideal playground for the children of the camp. There were long stretches of clean white sand and gravel to play in; Indian paint brush to suck honey from; thickets of wild roses, willow clumps for shade with violets hidden in the lush grass of their shady recesses, coral flowers and fragrant red mallow. An ideal spot also for two human vampires to find a childish victim!

'Not being on the main line of the railroad, that section was rarely visited by tramps at that time, although at long intervals they used the willows for a camping ground. Down there in the willows we assiduously cultivated the friendship of the little ones through stories we told them, and the judicious gifts of sweets. We finally decided upon a donor for the next transfusion operation in which Immortelle was to be the recipient. Carefully we spun the threads of our web.

'The Chaumelles were amongst the oldest and most respected residents of that section. There was no blood taint in the family. They had been clean-living and high-thinking people for generations. One of the children, Vernon, met all but one of the doctor's requirements. He possessed no trace of cruelty, and he was a hundred per cent perfect from a physical standpoint. He was courageous, strong-willed, but not stubborn, and of more than average mentality. He was then scarcely five years old and Linnie, his little sister and constant companion, was a little over three. They often came to play in the willows with older children. One day they ran away by themselves from their home at the opposite edge of town. They were playing in the grove near our house when Vernon fell and hurt his arm. It was a mere scratch and really needed no attention. By dint of a little candy and considerable persuasion, we succeeded in getting them inside the house, little golden-haired Linnie, with the wide, wondering blue eyes, and dark-eyed, sturdy little Vernon.

'Linnie was left in our living-room, while Immortelle *extracted the splinter* from her little brother's arm. A box of chocolates and some wondrously illustrated story books, purchased purposely for such occasions, occupied her attention for awhile; but tiring of them, she found her way unexpectedly, through a door carelessly left unlocked, to our subterranean operating room. I have never been able to forget the expression of her great blue eyes when she saw me in my white smock and cap, surrounded by the implements of my murderous occupation, and her little brother strapped securely to one table under the influence of the imperfect anesthetic, his pale face becoming ever paler as the life stream flowed from his little artery through the glass tube into the vein of the sinister-looking man reclining on the other table beside the child's couch. We were not yet using an aspirating syringe, which would allow us to measure the quantity of blood lost by the donor, and were alarmed by the pallor and weakness of the little boy. Even the two hardened creatures who assisted at the operation seemed frightened and conscience-stricken.

'I carried Vernon home, his little pale face resting on my shoulder. I had concocted some plausible tale to account for the prolonged absence of the children. The whole camp had been searching for them. I told a story of a fall and a wound caused by a piece of tin from an old can left by some hoboes at their camp, and a serious loss of blood. I promised to call next day and dress the wound in case it seemed inexpedient to take Vernon to the office. Dr Immortelle was indisposed, having injured himself with a lancet in dressing Vernon's wound. What a hypocrite I felt; how vile I knew myself to be, when they thanked me so profusely for my *kindness*!

'You know what happens sometimes to the best laid plans

of mice and men. Perhaps you recall the incident that led to our undoing; how Vernon's uncle, an eastern surgeon of some note, arrived unexpectedly on a visit and himself dressed the wound; how his suspicions were aroused. You remember how an infection developed and the child died, and how almost simultaneously the grave of a newborn infant was discovered in suspiciously close proximity to our "laboratory". Perhaps you can recall the investigation that followed. You may remember that a sort of catacombs was later discovered connecting with our operating-room, several bricked-up niches and their gruesome contents; but before that we were well on our way to safety. We owned one of the first automobiles in that part of the country.

'Your father declared that he had known Immortelle *himself* forty years before in the East, and not the latter's *father*, as Immortelle had always insisted; and to cap the climax, your grandfather solemnly averred that *he* had known this same Immortelle *sixty years before*, and that at the time he appeared in Wood River Valley, he appeared no older than at the time your grandfather had known him in his youth! One factor in his recognition and his positive identification consisted of a peculiar triangular scar over the left eyebrow. Had it been a birthmark it might have appeared for several generations; but it was improbable that three generations would meet with an accident resulting in the same identically shaped scar in the very same location. Some who had known your father and grandfather well for many years were frankly puzzled. They knew them for men whose reputation for truth and veracity had never been questioned. Others were greatly amused and openly accused them of being the victims of hallucinations. They made sarcastic references to the Wandering Jew, to St Germaine, to Lord Lytton's well-known hero, Zanoni, and that lesser-known but no less remarkable character of fiction, Melmuth the Wanderer.

'After some years we returned to San Francisco. Both of us were younger in appearance than when we fled from Idaho. Also, there were several little graves in the Argentine, whose occupants, if they could have spoken, might have thrown considerable light on the source of our youthful appearance and whose piteous tales would have wrung the hearts of humanity and brought down swift and terrible retribution on the vampires who had waxed young and strong on their suffering and the sacrifice of their young lives.

'It was not long until Immortelle was practicing successfully again, with a numerous and fashionable clientele. He soon acquired a reputation for philanthropy by contributing princely sums to various orphanages and other charitable institutions for children, and was always ready and willing to attend the little unfortunates they harbored, giving his services freely and without charge. Also, he did much charity work amongst the children of the poor, although not nearly so much as he was given credit for doing. I myself did a large portion of the work he was credited with. He was known to be deeply interested in the study of heredity and was a specialist in blood transfusion, which becomes increasingly safer, because of the continuous progress in aseptic surgery and the classification of humanity into groups according to the constituents of their blood.

'When at last his reputation seemed firmly established, he purchased an old house in the midst of a large, wooded acreage close to the ocean shore and within sound of the breakers, many miles south of the city. It had formerly belonged to an eccentric and wealthy recluse, who had chosen this secluded situation for his retirement. The advent of the automobile had changed conditions somewhat and a highway ran a comparatively short distance from the place. The house was an old, rambling structure. It stands on a rocky promontory overlooking the ocean, surrounded on two sides by a tall, thick cypress hedge. Little did the passing motorists dream of the stairs that led down through solid rock to a tunnel connecting with the ocean, and in which a stout boat was always moored.

'It was here that we established an orphanage and sanitarium for a small number of children, after thoroughly remodeling the old place. For these children Immortelle had conceived a deep and eternal interest and affection, but he sometimes remarked, with the most wistful expression and in an extremely melancholy tone, that no sooner had he become deeply attached to one of his young proteges than Fate would operate in some strange way to deprive him of their companionship – a fact which I thoroughly understood and was well able to confirm. He might also have added that Fate had seen fit to deprive him of the services of several nurses who had assisted at transfusion operations which had terminated unfortunately.

'Of course all our philanthropic efforts to avert disgrace did not terminate as we could desire. There were a number of mysterious disappearances of young women from that region which have never been explained to the satisfaction of – shall we use the stereotyped formula of "the police" or the "general public"? But in the public mind our own institution was never connected with them in any way until that accident in Deep Canyon.

'During the influenza epidemic, beautiful Linnie Chaumelle entered into our lives again, Linnie whom we had known as a child in Idaho and whose little brother Vernon had virtually met death at our hands. All the nurses in San Francisco were either in attendance on victims of the epidemic or ill themselves when it made its appearance at our orphanage. Linnie had chosen the career of a trained nurse. There is no finer or nobler under heaven. Her parents had both died when she was quite young and the family had become widely separated. Very likely she had forgotten the names of Immortelle and myself. Albert engaged her without a personal interview, contrary to his usual habit, on the recommendation of a brother physician. It was something we had never done before, but our need was urgent. When they met, it was obvious to me, who knew him so well, that with Dr Immortelle, the selfish, cynical, absolutely conscienceless man of the world, it was a case of love at first sight!

'It was not to be wondered at. Linnie Chaumelle is the most beautiful woman I have ever seen during more than a century and a half of evil living. She could well have served some great artist as the model for an angel, with her rose-leaf skin, her masses of chestnut hair with its glints of gold framing her lovely face; and those large, limpid blue eyes, through which one may glimpse her radiant soul.

'As time passed, it became increasingly evident that, for the first time in his evil existence, Albert had fallen victim to that little god who is no respecter of persons. Day by day I watched his love for Linnie grow. He vainly endeavored to exert his undoubtedly great hypnotic powers over her, but no evil power could affect that pure spirit that occupied a plane so vastly superior to his own. I had determined, in any event, that her mind should be kept free from the octopus-like tentacles of his hypnotic powers at any cost to myself.

'As I have said, all our philanthropic efforts did not terminate as successfully as we could have desired. It was while Linnie was at the sanitarium that one of the disastrous terminations occurred. Linnie is not naturally suspicious, but she is a young woman of more than average intelligence. As a nurse, she possesses from observation a wide knowledge of evil in countless manifestations; but her own soul has remained uncontaminated. She had not been there long before various circumstances combined to arouse her suspicions.

'I have mentioned a subterranean passage. It was convenient in case of emergency; and yet we found that stout ropes and even chains attached to pallid bodies of unfortunates and anchored by heavy weights have been snapped asunder by the violence of the breakers on that rocky coast. It was an incident of that nature that led to Immortelle's decision to dispose otherwise of the remains of a young and beautiful unfortunate and that likewise led to our undoing. Fate is a tricky hag! I should say, more correctly, what I now know to be the truth, that the time was at hand for reaping what we had sown.

'We had spent most of the previous night in digging a grave in the mellow soil of a small, isolated country place down the Peninsula. The ground belonged to me and I objected to this use of it, but my objections were silenced as usual by Immortelle. We removed the mute witness of our evil deeds from the sanitarium under cover of darkness, as we supposed, without the knowledge of any of the inmates except the one nurse attendant on that case. We had no reason to fear that she would make any damaging disclosures.

'Immortelle placed the poor body in the rear seat and sat beside it, supporting it in an upright position, while I drove the car. As I have said, he was by nature cowardly, and not all the transfusions from the veins of courageous donors had ever overcome this tendency. A large touring car followed us somewhat closely. Immortelle suspected that they had some suspicion of our sinister design, or that they might contemplate a hold-up. I think he was entirely wrong, but at any rate he became greatly agitated and was thrown into a perfect paroxysm of terror. His great black eyes rolled like the eyes of a maniac, his pallid face forming a startling contrast to his raven hair. His forehead was covered with great drops of perspiration and he was shaking as if with an ague. In any event, they could hardly have overtaken us. Our car was specially constructed for speed – as a physician's car should be, of course! Only we knew what speed it was capable of attaining. But he was terror-stricken, incapable of reasoning.

' "Faster! Faster," he screamed, as I drove the car at dangerous speed around sharp curves on the brink of a five-hundred-foot precipice. We managed to elude our pursuers, if such they were, by turning off into a little-used road and waiting until they had passed; then we turned back into the main road. Never have I seen a human being in such a panic. In spite of my remonstrances he made me stop as close to the brink as possible, where the canyon wall fell away below us for hundreds of feet, and compelled me to assist in pushing the poor girl's body over the edge into the abyss below. Then we re-entered the car and drove on to the city.

'In the ordinary course of events, the corpse would have remained undiscovered for years, perhaps until identification had become difficult, if not impossible; but in avoiding Scylla, we had become engulfed in Charybdis. Some Boy Scouts climbed down into the canyon next day to recover a lost hat and made the gruesome discovery of the remains!

'The papers were full of pictures of the poor victim who was not identified for a considerable space of time. They were full of supposed details of the crime. We felt comparatively safe, as only one of our nurses had been in attendance on the victim and we had every reason to feel sure of her discretion and loyalty. We had taken special precautions in regard to the arrival at the sanitarium of the girl now dead, so we felt confident that only the three of us had seen her there; but it happened that, of all persons in the world, Linnie had by accident, through the opening of the wrong door on a certain occasion obtained a passing glimpse of her and recognised her picture! She went to Immortelle at once. Her wonderful eyes rested steadily on his as she said:

' "I will ask you to take me to the city immediately, Dr Immortelle."

'He remonstrated, but it was useless, so he agreed that we

should take her in to the city that evening. Then he laid the hideous plan in which I apparently acquiesced.

' "She knows too much, now!" he said, his face distorted with rage and fear. "She must be silenced!" I shuddered. I had heard those words from him so many times in the course of close to a hundred and fifty years. I am certain he had come to feel the same towards me because of my increasing repugnance toward the course we were pursuing, which must have been obvious to him. My awakening conscience must have become a source of alarm to this man, himself without even the vestige of such an inconvenient faculty. I believe that he had planned my removal, as soon as it could be conveniently accomplished and he could secure the assistance of a confederate to take my place.

'We owned a cabin in a secluded nook, not far from the road, yet far enough to prevent any sounds of terror or agony from being heard by passing motorists. It had proven convenient for our purposes on more than one occasion. Its windows were heavily shuttered and it was surrounded by dense shrubs and trees, so that its existence would ordinarily have remained unsuspected by passers-by. Immortelle proposed that we should start for the city with Linnie. We were to develop engine trouble when opposite the cabin. Knowing that Linnie would not care to remain alone with him on the highway, such was the repugnance with which he evidently inspired her, I was to go to the cabin for the tools we should find necessary, and she was to accompany me. The rest would be easy, he judged from certain past experiences of a similar nature. After she had been drugged and rendered insensible and was at his mercy – after she had been kept at the pleasure of his will as long as suited his purpose, he judged she would become sufficiently tractable. Her own few remaining relatives were far away and she would probably not be missed for an indefinite period.

'I had an entirely different plan. I revered Linnie as I have never revered any other woman. I instinctively sensed the incorruptible purity of her soul, her unlimited sympathy of that maternal character which persists, though even in the very slightest degree, in the most debased and corrupted specimen of femininity. I would gladly have given my life to save her from him. I had no hope that she would ever care for me – no desire to bind her pure life to mine, with its innumerable crimes. I had ceased to crave for continued existence. The many crimes in which I had been Immortelle's accomplice, although for years unwillingly, lay heavy on my conscience. From myself the world had nothing more to fear; but the conscience of Immortelle was unawakened. He was a menace to humanity. I decided that the greatest service I could render humanity would be to put an end to his career, even at the sacrifice of my own life.

'We left the orphanage that evening after dinner. I was driving. Linnie occupied the seat beside me, refusing to sit in the rear seat with Immortelle, where, unknown to herself, only a short time before he had supported the body of a victim. Not far from the cabin that was to be her destination, and not far distant from the place where we had thrown the body of the young nurse over the canyon wall, I ran over a pedestrian. He was a tramp, clad in khaki-colored clothing – you know its low range of visibility – but we might have avoided striking him had it not been for the excessive speed at which we were traveling.

' "Drive on! Drive on, you fool!" screamed Immortelle as I stopped the car. All of us got out. The man was fatally injured but he still breathed.

' "Dead!" said Albert nonchalantly. He took the victim by the feet and dragged him out of the road.

' "Get in!" he ordered, as Linnie stood there, white with horror.

' "Surely you will not leave him there!" she gasped. "The man is not dead."

' "He is only a tramp! What difference can his life or death make?" snarled Immortelle.

' "He is a human being! If you leave him here you will leave me with him!" she said defiantly. The spotlight shone on Immortelle's face. It was black with rage and murderous. *And then Linnie remembered!*

' "I know you now, you fiend!" she said, and took a step nearer and shook her finger accusingly at him.

' *"You are the man who killed my little brother!"*

'Immortelle snarled like a trapped animal. There was the flash of steel in his hand; but before he could spring on Linnie with the knife, I had struck him on the head with a revolver. Then I trussed him up with a tow-rope and a dog-chain we had in the car. The tramp had breathed his last. I dragged both of them into the bushes. I put Linnie into the car.

' "I will return for them," I said in answer to her

unspoken question. We started for the nearest little railroad station, thinking she could catch the midnight local to the city. On the way I gave her the barest outline of this story. She is a nurse and acquainted with the marvelous results of transfusion, with all the latest aids and discoveries of the scientific medical world. Perhaps she thought me a mere madman, but I fully believe she accepted my story and had faith in my repentance. I made her promise to say nothing *until she should hear from me again.* I wanted to keep her name out of the papers. You know what they are. We had engine trouble in truth and it was late when we reached the outskirts of the little station where she was to take the train. Immortelle and myself and our car were well known there and I judged it best, in spite of the lateness of the hour, for her to proceed alone.

' "You will probably never see me again," I said at parting. "Think kindly of me sometimes, if you can."

' "Do not go back!" she begged. "I am afraid for you! He will kill you!"

'Perhaps she sensed that bit of good in me which persists in the most hardened. I had saved her. Perhaps she grasped my plan, telepathically, and shrank from its accomplishment, for her forebears have been law-abiding people for many generations. I took her hand and kissed it. The little innocent, with an impulse which sprang from her recognition of my genuine repentance, her gratitude, and her own strong maternal instinct of protection, put up her pure lips for me to kiss, she with her lily-white soul and I with my soul as black as my face once was! I was not fit to touch the hem of her garment with my lips, but I kissed her once. Nothing can erase the memory of that kiss. That second of supreme bliss was enough to recompense me for all I must face here and in the hereafter. I know you do not begrudge it to me, you who are destined to be her mate. Remember that, though I have practically become Aryan in body, my soul is still that of an Ethiopian – and colored people have strange moments of clairvoyance, whose reason is known only to the occultist.

'I drove away and left her. I have seen death in countless forms; I have been an accomplice, times without number, in what practically amounted to murder under the guise of scientific experimentation; I have witnessed scenes of horror whose remembrance fills me with an agony of remorse; and tears had been strangers to my eyes for what seemed like ages; but when I drove away and left her there, I could hardly see to drive for the blessed tears that filled my eyes. You know what happened – that she was too late for the local and started to walk to San Mateo, carrying her heavy suitcase. And how you came along and picked her up, thank God!

'I returned to the spot where I had left Immortelle and the body of the tramp. It makes cold chills run up and down my spine even now when I remember the look in Immortelle's eyes when I turned my flashlight on him where he lay bound and gagged. His eyes seemed to emit veritable flashes of venomous light. I almost quailed before him, bound and helpless as he was; but the thought of Linnie put courage into me. And I realised that my failure to carry out my plan meant death for me. My one fear was that someone would come along before my work was done, but there was little traffic over that road at night.

' "Now I am going to drive both of us over the cliff," I said. "If it were not for dragging *her* name through the mire, I would surrender myself and you to the authorities. But Justice is sometimes slow and uncertain. My plan seems the surest. I do not hold myself less guilty than yourself, although you were the greatest criminal in the beginning. However, I awoke, long ago, to the enormity of our crimes and would have endeavored to atone, in some measure, had you allowed me to do so. I have never been able to detect the slightest evidence of repentance in you. I wish it were possible for you to meet the fate you so richly deserve, in full possession of your faculties, but I dare not risk it. I shall be compelled to give you a few shots in the arm to insure your good behavior, for I shall have to unbind you to make the execution appear to be an accident." Almost it seemed that he would break even the stout chain in his frantic struggles to escape the awful fate that threatened. I drove the needle in deliberately, and often enough to render him incapable of resistance.

'I placed the tramp in the middle of the road. Then I lifted Immortelle into the machine, backed down the road some distance, came on at the rate of forty miles an hour or more, swerved the car as if in an effort to avoid running over the body of the tramp, and the next instant we were falling through space – down – down—

'You know how they picked up Immortelle, crushed and battered out of all semblance to his former self; how a tree broke my fall and they found me with my head and face unmarred, but with my back broken by the boulder I struck. Obviously, the papers all agreed, and I later corroborated them, that it was an accident due to the driver's swerving the car sharply in an effort to avoid running over the tramp. The most puzzling feature was the presence of a woman's footprints at the scene of the tragedy, a mystery which has never been solved! A possible solution was that the tramp had been struck by a hit-and-run woman motorist, who, finding that her car had killed the pedestrian, after getting out and examining him, had driven away and feared to report the accident.

'Immortelle's vast fortune will revert to the State, as he left no heirs. My own fortune I have left to be used for scientific and medical research, more especially with regard to blood transfusion and its free and scientific application for the benefit of suffering humanity.

'Sometimes as I lie here, I wonder if evil, or what we call by that name, *is* ever employed in the scheme of things for good ends. Can it be needed, like the substance we place at the roots of flowers to cause them to bloom more luxuriantly and more radiantly? Well, I shall soon know!' he said with that prescience of approaching death with which I was so soon to become familiar on the battlefields of France. He passed away that night.

Before I left him he made me promise to give his story to the world, believing that in proper hands, under scientific supervision, transfusion might prove of tremendous value to humanity; that it might be employed, not only to rejuvenate, but to repair and remedy both physical and mental defects. I have done my best. As I have said in the beginning, I am only a mining engineer, more familiar with the symbols of mineralogy and chemistry than with figures of speech.

Linnie and I both went across to France soon after our marriage. I remember the night we left San Francisco. There was no moon. The waters of the Bay were like a pool of black ink in which the vari-colored lights of the ships were reflected. To the south, a huge electric sign showed blood-colored through the smoke of some giant smokestack where men toiled in the sweat of their brows 'to make the world safe for Democracy!'

A wisp of smoke from a passing steamer was wrapped around the Ferry tower, almost concealing it, and above it the light on its summit shone like a symbol of Hope; but the Germans bombed the Red Cross tent where Linnie ministered to the sorely wounded! Although I escaped alive from the hell of the Argonne, I lie here almost as helpless as Victor de Lyle when I saw him last, longing for the time when my soul shall be reunited with its mate.